The Boy Without A Name
by
Idries Shah

HOOPOE BOOKS
BOSTON

Once upon a time, long, long, long ago, in a country
far from here, there lived a boy who had no name.
It is very strange to have no name, and you might ask,
"Why didn't he have a name?"

Well, it was like this.

On the day he was born, his parents were just about to choose a name for him when a very wise man came to the house.

"This is a very, very important boy," he told them, "and I am going to give him something marvelous one day, but I will have to give him his name first. So please don't give him a name yet."

"All right," said his parents, "but when will he get a name?"

"I cannot say now," replied the wise man, "but remember, he is a very important boy and you must be careful not to give him a name."

So the parents called him "Benaam," which means "Nameless" in the language of that country. For he was a boy without a name.

One day Nameless went to see his friend who lived in the next house. "Everybody has a name, and I would like to have one, too. Do you have a name you can give me?" he asked.

The other boy said, "I only have one name. It is Anwar. That's my name, and I need it. If I gave it to you, what would I do for a name? Besides, what would you give me if I did give you my name? You haven't got anything."

"I've got a dream I don't want. I could give you that," said Nameless.

"But how can we find out how to get a name and how to pass on a dream from one person to another?" asked Anwar.

"I know," replied Nameless, "let's go and ask the wise man!"

Now, the wise man knew everything, and fortunately he didn't live very far away.

So Nameless and Anwar went to his house and they knocked on the door. As soon as he saw them, the wise man said, "Come in, Nameless and Anwar!" even though he had never seen them before.

"How did you know who we were?" they asked.

"I know many things. And, besides, I was expecting you," said the wise man.

"Sit down here, and I'll see what I have in my magic boxes," he continued.

So the boys sat down on cushions beside the wise man.

And he took up a small box, saying, "This is a magic box, and it's absolutely full of all kinds of names. You just see."

And when he opened the lid of the box,
the boys could hear all the names in it.

There were all kinds of names. Names, names, names.
Names saying themselves, names saying other names.
Names saying names from all the countries of the world.

And the wise man picked a name out of the box and handed it to Nameless, and the name jumped onto his hand, ran up his arm and sprang onto his shoulder, and then it went into his ear and right into his head.

And suddenly he knew that he had a name!
"Hooray! Hooray!" he said, "I've got a name.
I am Husni!"

Husni was his name.

Then Anwar cried out, "But I want the dream that Husni promised me!"

"Patience, my boy!" said the wise man.

And he picked up another box and opened its lid. "This is a box of dreams that people don't want," he said. "You just stroke your head to take the dream out of it, Husni, and then put the dream into this box."

And Husni did so, and, sure enough, when he stroked his head he found that the dream came into his hand, and when he put his hand down near the box, the dream popped into the box.

Then the wise man took up another box, and he opened the lid and said, "This box is full of wonderful dreams!" And the two boys could see all sorts of marvelous dreams inside.

Wonderful, wonderful dreams!

"I am going to give you one dream each," said the wise man. And then he asked them each to pick a dream. And they did. And the dreams, as soon as they caught hold of them, ran up their arms, onto their shoulders, into their ears and right into their heads, just as Husni's name had done.

And after that, forever and ever,
Husni had a name ...

and the two boys, Husni and Anwar, always had wonderful dreams.